Workitu's PASSOVER

A Story from Ethiopia

Written by Zahava Workitu Goshen
& Maayan Ben Hagai

Illustrations by Eden Spivak
Translated by Jessica Bonn

Green Bean Books

The morning sounds of the village drifted in through Workitu's window: a cow mooing, leaves blowing in the breeze, and the clicking of her mother's pestle and mortar.

Workitu was sitting on her bed. It was time for breakfast, but she didn't move, even when her mother called for her.

"Where's Workitu?" her little sister, Almaz, asked. "I'll go see."

A moment later, the smiling face of Almaz peeked in through the doorway.

"Come on! The sun's already up!" she said. "And today's a big day."

But Workitu stayed on her bed. "I don't want to get up, and I don't want to wear that old dress," she said, looking at a faded dress draped over a chair.

"Oh, don't be sad!" said Almaz. "It's almost Passover, remember? Abba is weaving us new dresses. They'll be as white as milk!"

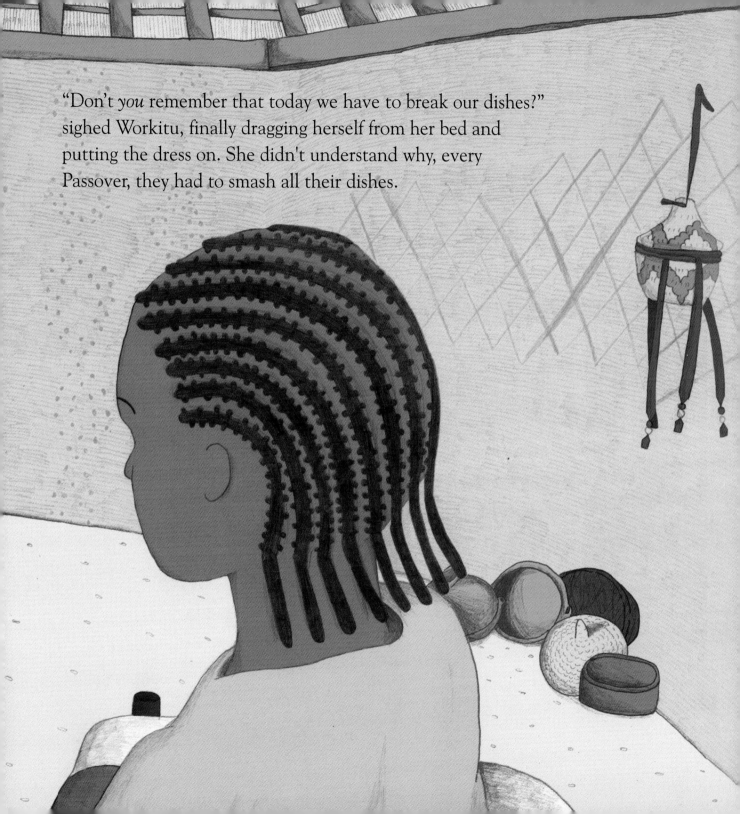

"Don't *you* remember that today we have to break our dishes?" sighed Workitu, finally dragging herself from her bed and putting the dress on. She didn't understand why, every Passover, they had to smash all their dishes.

"Hurry up!" urged their mother. "Auntie Balainesh is waiting for you at her hut."

But Workitu didn't rush. She held her favorite cup tightly and sipped her milk very, *very* slowly.

Almaz's arms were already full of bowls and other things she'd collected, and Ima carefully balanced a water jar on top of her head. "Are you ready, Workitu?" Ima asked.

"I guess," said Workitu. She kept hold of her cup and took a large pot from the floor. It had round handles like big ears, and she loved everything her mother made in it.

Workitu didn't find it easy walking to her
auntie's hut with her cup and a heavy pot in her hands.
    "Don't drop anything," she called out to her little sister.
    "Why not?" laughed Almaz. "We're going to break
them anyway!"

Outside her hut, Auntie Balainesh was mixing deep red clay with water.

"Your face is all dirty, Auntie!" cried Almaz.

"Soon yours will be too!" said their auntie.
"But first it's time to break your dishes!"
    She pointed to the flat rock next to her.

Workitu clasped her pot and cup tightly. She didn't want to smash anything.

"Come on, child," said Auntie Balainesh. "It's time to break everything from last year. Throw them hard; don't hold back! Think of all the *chametz* they carry."

Suddenly there was a loud crash. Almaz had hurled her armful of dishes onto the rock.

Startled, Workitu dropped her favorite cup and watched it shatter. Tears rolled down her cheeks and fell onto the cup's broken pieces.

Letting her pot fall too, she ran off.

"Workitu, come back!" Almaz cried.

Auntie Balainesh found Workitu curled up behind a bush, her cheeks wet.

"Do you know," her auntie said gently, "that when I was a child I used to break things all the time? Not just for Passover, but all year long! Your grandma said I must have holes in my hands!"

"One day, when I broke her favorite bowl, she just looked at me and said, 'Balainesh, it's time to teach you how to make new things from everything you break.'"

Auntie Balainesh walked Workitu back to the hut.

"But why must you break all the beautiful things you and Ima have made?" Workitu asked.

"We must break old things to make room for the new. We break, but then we make again. Both with the same hands."

Auntie Balainesh took a large stone and crushed the shards of Workitu's broken cup into tiny pieces.

"Sometimes it's good to let go of old things. Like saying goodbye to your baby teeth."

Workitu remembered how it felt when a new tooth poked up from where the old one used to be. Maybe the world was like that — new things always pushing through.

"Crush each piece until it becomes like flour," Auntie Balainesh told the girls, handing Workitu a fist-sized stone. "Imagine this stone is your pestle and the flat rock is your mortar."

Workitu tapped the shard gently — she still didn't want to break things.

"Why do they need to be in such tiny pieces?" she asked.

"So we can turn them back into pots and cups," Auntie replied.

"But how?"

"Watch and you will see!"

Workitu smashed the shards. Then she ground them up, just like Auntie showed her. It all turned into a fine powder.

Auntie Balainesh added the fine powder from the broken pots to some wet clay. She mixed them together and started kneading.

Watching her auntie work, Workitu felt excited. Her old things were secretly hidden inside the clay they were using to make new things. And when the new pots were ready, Passover would be here. It was like her auntie's moving hands were tugging at the holiday, pulling it into their little village.

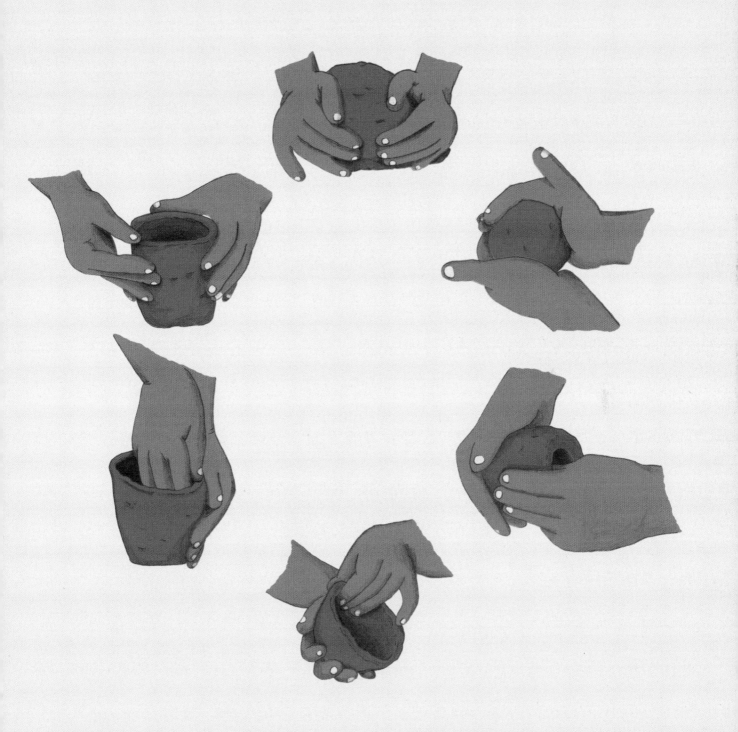

Following her auntie's instructions, Workitu shaped her clay. She thought about Ima and Auntie doing the same when they were girls.

"Wait!" Workitu gasped. "Does this mean that all of your pots — and Grandma's and even Great-Grandma's — were made again and again from this same clay?"

"Yes!" said her auntie, laughing.

So the clay is ancient, thought Workitu. *Maybe it's even from the time when the Jewish people left Egypt.*

She rolled the red-brown clay into a ball, hollowing it out with her thumbs. Using her fingers, she pinched part of it into a little nose. She made the handle just like an ear. Perhaps Abba could use it as a jug to hold the oil from their olive trees.

The sun started to set, turning the new stew pots, water jugs, cups, and bowls they'd made to a deep orange.

"By tomorrow evening, these will be dry," Auntie Balainesh declared. "Then we'll bake them in a hot fire to make them even stronger!"

Auntie Balainesh lifted Workitu's oil jar from among the pieces they'd made, examining it carefully. "Workitu, you are very talented. I am so proud of you."

Workitu smiled. She couldn't wait to show Ima what she'd made from her favorite cup and pot.

As Workitu lay in bed that night, the almost-full moon peered in through her window. Passover was just around the corner, and her new dress, whiter than milk, lay on the chair. She drifted off to sleep, imagining the moon as a huge ball of clay in the night sky.

Workitu's Passover is a tale based on the childhood memories of Zahava Workitu Goshen, who grew up in a small Jewish village in the Gondar region of Ethiopia and immigrated to Israel with her family in 1984. It introduces us to some of the Passover customs of Beta Israel, the Jews of Ethiopia.

Before the holiday, Ethiopian Jews would break up their clay kitchenware, which had been used throughout the year. These fragments were then blended with moist clay, and then new containers were crafted from the mixture. The pieces were decorated, then fired in a kiln.

As shown in *Workitu's Passover,* another tradition was to make new clothes for family members in honor of Passover. Zahava's father was a skilled weaver who crafted beautiful clothes for Zahava, which her mother embroidered with exquisite decorations.

First published in 2022 by Asia Publishing
First published in the UK in 2024 by Green Bean Books
c/o Pen & Sword Books Ltd
George House, Unit 12 & 13, Beevor Street, Off Pontefract Road, Barnsley, South Yorkshire S71 1HN
www.greenbeanbooks.com

Green Bean Books edition: 978-1-78438-899-7
Harold Grinspoon Foundation edition: 978-1-78438-989-5

Translated by Jessica Bonn
Designed by Ian Hughes
Edited by Alli Brydon, Lisa Silverman and Rachael Stein
Production by Hugh Allan

Printed in China by Imago
0324/B2484/A7